•Abente s•

Ein Besuch bei Großmutter

•Adventures with Nicholas•
A Visit to Grandma

Illustrated by Chris L. Demarest

Berlitz Kids™
Berlitz Publishing Company, Inc.

Princeton   Mexico City   Dublin
          Eschborn   Singapore

Dear Parents,

The *Adventures with Nicholas* stories will create hours of fun and productive learning for you and your child. Children love sharing books with adults, and story-based learning is a natural way for your child to develop second language skills in an enjoyable and entertaining way.

In 1878, Professor Maximilian Berlitz had a revolutionary idea about making language learning accessible and enjoyable. These same principles are still successfully at work today. Now, more than a century later, people all over the world recognize and appreciate his successful approach. Berlitz Kids combines the time-honored traditions of Professor Berlitz with current research to create superior products that truly help children learn and enjoy foreign languages.

Berlitz Kids materials let your child gain access to a second language in a positive and engaging way. The eight episodes in this book present foreign language words gradually, and help children build vocabulary naturally. The content and vocabulary have been carefully chosen by language experts to draw your child into the action. Within a short time, your child may be repeating parts of the story in the new language! What fun for you and your child!

Another bonus of the *Adventures with Nicholas* materials is that they are portable. The small book and cassette are easy to use at home, in the car, or even on a visit to a grandma's house! Each of the books in the Nicholas series emphasizes slightly different vocabulary and concepts; taken together, the series encourages learning all the time.

The audio cassette is designed for easy use. The eight stories, accompanied by entertaining sound effects and a special audio dictionary, are on Side 1. Eight delightful songs, which are linked thematically to the stories, are on Side 2. Current research shows that singing songs helps children learn the sounds of a new language more easily…and your child will enjoy hearing and singing these memorable songs over and over again.

Follow your child's lead as you work through the wonderful stories and songs. And above all, enjoy yourselves.

Welcome!

The Editors at Berlitz Kids

Nikolaus erinnert sich

Nicholas Remembers

Nikolaus denkt an seine Großmutter.

Nicholas is thinking about his grandma.

Als Nikolaus drei Jahre alt war, schenkte ihm Großmutter lustige Spielsachen.

When Nicholas was three years old, Grandma gave him funny toys.

„Danke schön, Großmutter. Ich hab'
dich lieb", sagte Nikolaus.

„Ich hab' dich auch lieb", sagte
Großmutter.

"Thank you, Grandma. I love you," said Nicholas.
"I love you, too," said Grandma.

Als Nikolaus vier Jahre alt war, fiel er hin.
Großmutter klebte ihm ein Pflaster aufs
Knie. Sie umarmte ihn. Und bald schon
fühlte er sich viel besser.

When Nicholas was four years old, he fell down.
Grandma put a bandage on his knee. She hugged him.
And soon he felt much better.

Als Nikolaus fünf Jahre alt war, sang
Großmutter Lieder mit ihm. Sie lachten
und hatten sehr viel Spaß.

*When Nicholas was five years old, Grandma
sang songs with him. They laughed and had a
wonderful time.*

Jetzt ist Nikolaus älter und größer.
Heute denkt er an Großmutter. Morgen hat
Großmutter Geburtstag. Er möchte seiner
Großmutter etwas Wunderschönes schenken!

*Now Nicholas is older and bigger. Today
he is thinking about Grandma. Tomorrow is
Grandma's birthday. He wants to give his grandma
a wonderful present!*

② Was für ein Geschenk?

What Present?

Nikolaus, sein Bruder Hans und seine
Schwester Maria sitzen im Wohnzimmer.
Sie reden darüber, was sie Großmutter zum
Geburtstag kaufen können.

*Nicholas, his brother John, and his sister Maria
sit in the living room. They talk about what to buy for
Grandma's birthday.*

„Kaufen wir Blumen", sagt Maria.
„Großmutter liebt Blumen. Sie liebt
große und kleine, lange und kurze,
rosa, rote und weiße Blumen."

*"Let's buy flowers," says Maria. "Grandma
loves flowers. She loves big and small, tall and
short, pink, red, and white flowers."*

„Ja", sagt Nikolaus. „Aber Großmutter hat schon einen großen Garten. Sie hat schon so viele Blumen."

"Yes," says Nicholas. "But Grandma already has a big garden. She already has so many flowers."

„Kaufen wir doch Parfüm", sagt Nikolaus.
„Parfüm riecht so gut."

„Ja", sagt Maria. „Aber Großmutter hat
schon so viel Parfüm."

*"Let's buy perfume," says Nicholas. "Perfume
smells so good."*

*"Yes," says Maria. "But Grandma already has so
much perfume."*

„Kaufen wir eben eine Schachtel Pralinen",
sagt Hans. „Pralinen schmecken so gut."
„Ja", sagt Nikolaus. „Aber Großmutter
isst nicht gern zuviele Süßigkeiten."

"Let's buy a box of chocolates," says John.
"Chocolate tastes so good."
"Yes," says Nicholas. "But Grandma does not
like to eat too many sweets."

Nikolaus lässt den Kopf hängen. Er macht sich Sorgen. Er weiß nicht, was sie Großmutter kaufen sollen.

Nicholas puts his head in his hands. He is worried.
He does not know what to buy for Grandma.

3 Im Geschäft

At the Store

Am nächsten Tag gehen die Kinder mit Mutti einkaufen.

„Ich weiß!", sagt Nikolaus. „Kaufen wir doch einen Hut für Großmutter. Großmutter mag Hüte."

„Was für eine gute Idee!", sagt Mutti.

The next day the children go shopping with Mom.
"I know!" says Nicholas. "Let's buy a hat for Grandma. Grandma likes hats."
"What a good idea!" says Mom.

„Guten Morgen", sagt eine Frau.
„Guten Morgen", sagen Mutti und
die Kinder.

"Good morning," says a woman.
"Good morning," say Mom and the children.

„Wir möchten einen Hut kaufen",
sagt Nikolaus.
„Für dich?", fragt die Frau.
Sie setzt Nikolaus einen roten Hut auf.
„Nein, nicht für mich", sagt Nikolaus.

"We want to buy a hat," says Nicholas.
"For you?" asks the woman.
She puts a red hat on Nicholas.
"No, not for me," says Nicholas.

„Für dich?", fragt die Frau.
Sie setzt Maria einen grünen und
lilafarbenen Hut auf.
„Nein, nicht für mich", sagt Maria.

"For you?" asks the woman.
She puts a green and purple hat on Maria.
"No, not for me," says Maria.

„Für dich?", fragt die Frau.
Sie setzt Hans einen gelben Hut auf.

"For you?" asks the woman.
She puts a yellow hat on John.

„Nein, nicht für mich", sagt Hans. „Für
unsere Großmutter!"

"No, not for me," says John. "For our grandma!"

Sie schauen sich orange Hüte, blaue Hüte und schwarze Hüte an. Einen passenden Hut für Großmutter sehen sie nicht. Sie sind traurig.

They look at orange hats, blue hats, and black hats. They do not see a good hat for Grandma. They feel sad.

„Ich habe eine Idee", sagt Nikolaus.
Er flüstert seiner Familie etwas zu. Alle
strahlen und sagen: „Ja!"

"I have an idea," says Nicolas.
He whispers to his family. Everyone smiles and
says, "Yes!"

Nikolaus hofft, dass Großmutter seine
Idee mag.

Nicolas hopes Grandma likes his idea.

Vorbereitungen

Getting Ready

Es wird Zeit, sich für Großmutters Geburtstagsparty fertig zu machen. Jeder will gut aussehen – sogar die Katzen, Prinzessin und Kätzchen.

It is time to get ready for Grandma's birthday party. Everyone wants to look good—even the cats, Princess and Kitten.

Mutti bürstet sich die Haare.

Mom brushes her hair.

Vati bindet sich die Krawatte um.

Dad ties his tie.

25

Hans wäscht sich das Gesicht.

John washes his face.

Maria bügelt ihr rotes Kleid.

Maria irons her red dress.

Nikolaus zieht sich ein weißes Hemd,
blaue Hosen und neue braune Schuhe an.

*Nicholas puts on a white shirt, blue pants, and
new brown shoes.*

Die Kinder stecken sich kleine
Geschenke in die Taschen. Und dann sind
sie fertig zum Besuch bei Großmutter.

The children put little presents in their pockets.
And then they are ready for a visit to Grandma.

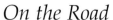

Auf der Straße

On the Road

Sie laufen zum Auto und steigen ein. Vati sitzt vorne hinter dem Lenkrad. Mutti sitzt neben Vati.

They run to the car and get in. Dad sits in the front, behind the wheel. Mom sits next to Dad.

Die Kinder sitzen hinten. Nikolaus sitzt rechts von Hans. Maria sitzt links von Hans.

The children sit in the back. Nicholas sits to the right of John. Maria sits to the left of John.

Kätzchen sitzt unter den Beinen von Maria. Prinzessin schläft auf dem Schoß von Hans.

Kitten sits under Maria's legs. Princess sleeps on John's lap.

Es ist sehr voll im Auto. Dann fängt
Mutti an zu singen, und alle machen mit.

The car is very crowded. Then Mom starts to sing,
and everyone joins in.

Die Lieder sind lustig. Sie lachen alle
und haben Spaß.

*The songs are funny. They all laugh and have a
good time.*

Nikolaus singt mit. Aber dann macht er sich wieder Sorgen.

„Ich hoffe nur, dass Großmutter unsere Geschenke mag", sagt er.

Nicholas sings, too. But then he feels worried again.
"I just hope Grandma likes our presents," he says.

Bei Großmutter zu Hause

At Grandma's House

Alle Gäste sind bei Großmutter zu Hause. Sie hat eine große Familie und viele, viele Freunde. Sie alle kommen zu ihrer Geburtstagsparty.

All the guests are at Grandma's house. She has a big family and many, many friends. All of them come to her birthday party.

Es gibt einen großen Kuchen mit Kerzen.
Es gibt Eis.

There is a big cake with candles. There is ice cream.

Es gibt Partyhüte für alle. Und es gibt
fröhliche Musik.

*There are party hats for everyone. And there is
happy music.*

Großmutter bekommt viele Geschenke.
Sie bekommt Farben und Pinsel, um Bilder
zu malen.

*Grandma gets many presents. She gets paints and
brushes to paint pictures.*

Sie bekommt eine Kamera, um Photos zu machen, wenn sie an weit entfernte Orte reist. Sie bekommt ein leeres Buch, um ihre Lebensgeschichte zu schreiben.

She gets a camera to take photographs when she goes to faraway places. She gets a blank book to write the story of her life.

„Danke schön", sagt Großmutter.
Dann stehen Nikolaus, Maria und Hans
auf. Alle sehen die Kinder an.

"Thank you," says Grandma.
Then Nicholas, Maria, and John stand up.
Everyone looks at the children.

Mehr Geschenke

More Presents

„Wir haben auch Geschenke für dich",
sagt Nikolaus.
    Großmutter lächelt.

"We have presents for you, too," says Nicholas.
Grandma smiles.

Nikolaus geht ans Klavier. Er spielt ein
fröhliches Lied. Er spielt es schnell und laut.

Nicholas goes to the piano. He plays a happy song.
He plays it fast and loud.

Maria tanzt im Zimmer herum.
Prinzessin und Kätzchen tanzen mit.

*Maria dances around the room. Princess and
Kitten dance, too.*

Hans steht auf dem Kopf. Er singt ein
Lied . . . mit dem Kopf nach unten.

John stands on his head. He sings a song . . .
upside-down.

Prinzessin und Kätzchen versuchen
mitzusingen.

Princess and Kitten try to sing, too.

Alle klatschen und jubeln – besonders
Großmutter.

Everyone claps and cheers—especially Grandma.

Nikolaus sagt: „Ich freue mich, dass du
die Aufführung magst, Großmutter. Jetzt
haben wir noch eine Überraschung für dich."

*Nicholas says, "I'm glad you like the show,
Grandma. Now, we have one more surprise for you."*

Die letzte Überraschung

The Last Surprise

Nikolaus, Maria und Hans holen die
Geschenke aus ihren Taschen. Die Geschenke
sehen wie kleine Herzen aus.

*Nicholas, Maria, and John take the presents out of
their pockets. The presents look like little hearts.*

Großmutter öffnet das Geschenk von
Maria. Es ist ein Photo von Maria, als sie ein
Baby war.

Grandma opens Maria's present. It is a
photograph of Maria when she was a baby.

Auf dem Photo spielen Großmutter
und Maria mit einem lustigen Spielzeug.
Unter dem Photo steht: „Ich hab' dich
lieb, Großmutter."

In the photo, Grandma and Maria are playing
with a funny toy. Under the photo, it says "I love
you, Grandma."

Großmutter öffnet das Geschenk von
Hans. Es ist ein Photo von Hans, als er ein Baby
war. Auf dem Photo klebt Großmutter Hans
ein Pflaster auf den Arm. Unter dem Photo
steht: „Ich hab' dich lieb, Großmutter."

*Grandma opens John's present. It is a photograph
of John when he was a baby. In the photo, Grandma is
putting a bandage on John's arm. Under the photo, it
says "I love you, Grandma."*

Großmutter sieht sich das Geschenk von Nikolaus an. Auf dem Photo singen Nikolaus und Großmutter. Sie lachen und haben sehr viel Spaß. Unter dem Photo steht: „Ich hab' dich lieb, Großmutter."

Grandma looks at Nicholas's present. In the photo, Nicholas and Grandma are singing. They are laughing and having a wonderful time. Under the photo, it says, "I love you, Grandma."

Ich hab' dich lieb, Großmutter

Großmutter strahlt und umarmt die
drei Kinder.

„Ich mag die Farben und Pinsel. Ich mag
die Kamera. Ich mag das Buch. Und ich
mag eure Aufführung. Aber am allermeisten mag
ich die Photos . . . weil es Photos von
euch sind."

Grandma smiles and hugs the three children.
"I like the paints and brushes. I like the camera. I
like the book. And I like your show. But most of all, I
like the photos . . . because they are photos of you."

Nikolaus, Maria und Hans sind sehr glücklich.
„Ich hab' euch alle lieb", sagt Großmutter.
„Wir haben dich auch lieb", sagen die Kinder.

Nicholas, Maria, and John are very happy.
"I love you all," says Grandma.
"We love you, too," say the children.

Dann zählt Nikolaus: „Eins, zwei,
drei . . ." Und alle sagen: „Alles Gute zum
Geburtstag, Großmutter!"

Then Nicholas counts, "One, two, three . . . "
And everyone says, "Happy birthday, Grandma!"

Song Lyrics

Song to Accompany Story 1

Meine Familie *(My Family)*

[Sung to the melody of a French folk tune]

Vater, Mutter, Schwester, Bruder –
Das ist meine Familie. Meine Familie.
Ich sag' dir, was die tun
    ist schrecklich albern.
Das ist wahr.

Father, Mother, Sister, Brother,
That's my family. That's my family.
I tell you what they do—
    is very silly
That is true!

Vater nimmt seine zahme Schlange
Ins Büro mit, ins Büro mit.
Die Schlange, die Schneeflocke heißt,
Macht Vatis Arbeit fehlerlos.

Father takes—his pet snake,
To the office, to the office.
That pet snake, named Snowflake,
Does Dad's work with no mistakes.

Mutter backt Grünebohnenkuchen,
Jeden Morgen, jeden Morgen.
Ich bin bös, denn sie schmecken schlecht.
Doch sind sie weg, freu ich
    mich echt.

Mother bakes—stringbean cakes,
Every morning, every morning.
I am mad 'cause they taste bad.
But when they're gone,
    I'm really glad.

Schwester geht spazieren gern
Mit ihrer Schildkröte, mit ihrer Schildkröte.
Wohin sie gehen, weiß ich nicht,
Doch langsam laufen sie bestimmt.

Sister likes—to take hikes
With her turtle, with her turtle.
Where they go, I don't know,
But I'm sure that they walk slow.

Bruder isst mit den Füßen.
Das wirkt komisch, das wirkt komisch.
Wenn er etwas Leckres isst,
Tut er's nur im Sitzen.

Brother eats with his feet.
He looks funny; he looks funny.
When he eats any treats,
He must sit and take a seat.

[Repeat first verse.]

[Repeat first verse.]

Song to Accompany Story 2

Ach, was tun wir nur? *(Oh, What Can We Do?)*

[Sung to the melody of a Spanish folk tune]

Ach, was tun wir nur zum Geburtstag
    von Oma?
Ach, was können wir zu ihrem
    Ehrentag tun?
Hol'n wir ihr 'nen Frosch, der spricht,
Einen, der gern wandern geht.
So was können wir zum Tag von
    Oma tun.

Oh, what can we do for our
    grandmother's birthday?
Oh, what can we do for her
    special day?
We can get a frog that talks—
One that likes to go for walks.
That's what we can do for our
    grandma's day.

Ach, was tun wir nur zum Geburtstag
  von Oma?
Ach, was können wir zu ihrem
  Ehrentag tun?
Hol'n wir ihr ein Pferd, das lacht –
Hier, schau Photos von ihm an. Und . . .

Oh, what can we do for our
  grandmother's birthday?
Oh, what can we do for her
  special day?
We can get a horse that laughs—
Here, look at his photographs. And . . .

Ach, was tun wir nur zum Geburtstag
  von Oma?
Ach, was können wir zu ihrem
  Ehrentag tun?
Hol'n wir ihr 'ne Kuh, die hüpft –
Eine mit komischem Maul, vielleicht. Und . . .

Oh, what can we do for our
  grandmother's birthday?
Oh, what can we do for her
  special day?
We can get a cow that skips—
Maybe one with funny lips. And . . .

Ach, was tun wir nur zum Geburtstag
  von Oma?
Ach, was können wir zu ihrem
  Ehrentag tun?
Hol'n wir ihr 'nen Fisch, der Ski läuft –
Ich kenn' einen, der Luise heißt. Und . . .

Oh, what can we do for our
  grandmother's birthday?
Oh, what can we do for her
  special day?
We can get a fish that skis—
I know one who's named Louise. And . . .

Ach, was tun wir nur zum Geburtstag
  von Oma?
Ach, was können wir zu ihrem
  Ehrentag tun?
Hol'n wir ihr ein Schwein, das weiß,
Wie man Garderobe näht. Und . . .
All das können wir zum Tag von
  Oma tun.

Oh, what can we do for our
  grandmother's birthday?
Oh, what can we do for her
  special day?
We can get a pig that knows
How to sew a suit of clothes. And . . .
We can do all this for our
  grandma's day!

Song to Accompany Story 3

Eine bunte Welt *(A Colorful World)*
[Sung to the melody of a German folk tune]

Stell dir den Himmel mal leuchtend
  gelb vor –
Mit roten Wolken und blauen Wolken, und
Grünen Flugzeugen, die fliegen vorbei.
Oh, wär das nicht eine schöne, bunte Welt!

Can you imagine a bright
  yellow sky—
With red clouds and blue clouds and
Green airplanes flying by?
Oh, what a colorful world this would be!

Stell dir das Meer doch mal violett vor –
Mit roten Fischen und blauen Fischen, und
Braunen Schildkröten, die
  schwimmen vorbei.
Oh, wär das nicht eine schöne, bunte Welt!

Can you imagine a violet sea—
With red fish and blue fish and
Brown turtles
  swimming by?
Oh, what a colorful world this would be!

Stell dir die Autobahn mal aus Gold vor –
Mit roten Autos und blauen Autos, und
Weißen Bussen, die fahren vorbei.
Oh, wär das nicht eine schöne, bunte Welt!

Can you imagine a highway of gold—
With red cars and blue cars and
White buses driving by?
Oh, what a colorful world this would be!

Stell dir den Strand einmal in Lila vor –
Mit roten Muscheln und blauen
    Muscheln, und
Orangen Krebsen, die krabbeln vorbei.
Oh, wär das nicht eine schöne, bunte Welt!

[Repeat first verse.]

Can you imagine a dark purple beach—
With red shells and blue
    shells and
Orange crabs crawling by?
Oh, what a colorful world this would be!

[Repeat first verse.]

Song to Accompany Story 4

Bist du fertig? *(Are You Ready?)*

[Sung to the tune of "Twinkle, Twinkle, Little Star"]

Willst du eine Reise machen?
Erlaub mir ein paar kleine Tips.
Erst füll die Wanne. Tu dein
    Entlein rein.
Ein Bad macht Spaß, da hast du Glück.
Spring nur rein – es ist nicht zu heiß.
Schwimm herum und plansch recht viel.

Are you ready for a trip?
Let me give you little tips.
First fill the tub. Add your
    toy duck.
A bath is fun, so you're in luck.
Jump right in—it's not too hot.
Swim around, and splash a lot.

Dann steig raus und tropf, tropf, tropf.
Versuch nicht auszurut–sch–en.
Doch ein Handtuch und trockne dir den Bauch.
Mach mal Pause – probier' ein Geleebrot.
Kämm dein Haar, damit's nett wirkt.
Strubblig ist's, drum mach es zweimal.

Then get out and drip, drip, drip.
Just try not to slip, slip, slip.
Get a towel and dry your belly.
Take a break—try bread and jelly.
Comb your hair, so it looks nice.
It's a mess, so do it twice.

Doch hol dir Kleider. Was ziehst du an?
Mach schon zu! Ganz nackt bist du.
Zieh dich schnell an,– es ist sechs
    Uhr neunzehn!
Wähl ein Hemd. Nimm eins, das sauber ist.
Denk dran, deine Schuhe zu finden.
Die sind was, was du oft verlierst.

Get your clothes. What can you wear?
Hurry up! You're very bare.
Get dressed fast—it's
    six nineteen!
Choose a shirt. Take one that's clean.
Don't forget to find your shoes.
Those are things you often lose.

Bist du fertig? Halt, denk nach!
Vielleicht solltest du was zu trinken packen.
Es ist schon spät,– du fährst ja weit.
Gleich geht's los,– steig in das Auto!
Schließ die Tür und schau hinaus,
Jetzt sind wir zur Fahrt bereit!

Are you ready? Stop and think.
Maybe you should pack a drink.
It's getting late—you're going far.
It's time to run—get in the car.
Close the door, and look outside,
Now we're ready for a ride!

Song to Accompany Story 5

Gebt mir ein Heim (*Give me a Home*)

[Sung to the tune of "Home on the Range"]

Ach, gebt mir ein Heim,
Wo mein Zebra laufen kann,
Ein Heim mit einem großen Wohnzimmer!
Es kann die Füße hochlegen,
Während ich ihm Leckeres bring,
Und die Krümel mit dem Besen aufkehr'.

[Chorus]

Heim, Heim, trautes Heim,
Für mich und das Zebra so lieb.
Unsre Tage sind schön,
Und ich sage es gern,
Jeder Raum ist ein Raum voller Freud'.

Ach, gebt mir ein Heim,
Wo mein Zebra laufen kann,
Und im Schlafzimmer dort wird
 es schnarchen!
Auf dem Bett da schläft es,
Während ich ihm den Kopf kraul';
Ich selbst schlafe halt auf dem Boden.

[Repeat chorus.]

Ach, gebt mir ein Heim,
Wo mein Zebra laufen kann.
In der Küche koch' ich, was es wünscht.
Ich mach' Kuchen und Salat
Diesem Zebra zulieb',
Wenn es sagt, es hilft mit dem Geschirr.

[Repeat chorus.]

Oh, give me a home
Where my zebra can roam,
A place with a big living room.
He can put up his feet
While I bring him a treat,
And sweep up his crumbs with a broom.

[*Chorus*]

Home, home, sweet home,
For me and the zebra so dear.
We have wonderful days,
And I'm happy to say
That each room is a room full of cheer.

Oh, give me a home
Where my zebra can roam,
And there in the bedroom
 he'll snore.
He can sleep on the bed,
While I scratch his big head;
As for me, I can sleep on the floor.

[*Repeat chorus.*]

Oh, give me a home,
Where my zebra can roam.
In the kitchen I'll cook what he wishes.
I'll make salad and cake
For that dear zebra's sake,
If he says he will help with the dishes.

[*Repeat chorus.*]

Song to Accompany Story 6

Laden wir alle ein (*Let's Invite Everyone*)

[Sung to the melody of an American folk tune]

Machen wir eine Party!
Haben wir ein bisschen Spaß!
Ich frag' Mutter.
Frag' du Vati.
Laden wir alle ein!

We can have a party.
We can have some fun.
I'll ask Mother.
You ask Dad.
Let's invite everyone!

Wer kommt auf unsere Party?	Who is coming to our party?
Wer will ein bisschen Spaß?	Who wants to have some fun?
Ruf den großen, braunen Bären	Call the big brown bear,
Mit dem lockigen Pelz.	With the curly hair.
Laden wir alle ein!	Let's invite everyone!

Wer kommt auf unsere Party?	Who is coming to our party?
Wer will ein bisschen Spaß?	Who wants to have some fun?
Hol die große Giraffe.	Get the tall giraffe.
Sie ist zum Lachen. . . .	She makes us laugh. . . .

Wer kommt auf unsere Party?	Who is coming to our party?
Wer will ein bisschen Spaß?	Who wants to have some fun?
Find' die lustige Ziege	Find the funny goat,
Mit dem tollen, dicken Fell. . . .	With the great, big coat. . . .

Wer kommt auf unsere Party?	Who is coming to our party?
Wer will ein bisschen Spaß?	Who wants to have some fun?
Frag' den tanzenden Fuchs,	Ask the dancing fox,
Der schicke Socken trägt. . . .	Who wears fancy socks. . . .
Das müssen, glaub' ich, alle sein.	I think that is everyone!

Song to Accompany Story 7

Eine Party *(A Party)*

[Sung to the melody of an Italian folk tune]

'ne Party! 'ne Party!	A party! A party!
Wir machen 'ne Party.	We're having a party.
Wir können essen und singen!	We can eat and sing!
Und hier ist, was ich bring':	And this is what I will bring:
Klopse, Spaghetti,	Meatballs, spaghetti,
Rotes und blaues Konfetti,	Red and blue confetti,
Frisch gebratenen Fisch	Fresh fried fish,
Mit 'ner Schale saurer Gurken.	With pickles in a dish.

Erdnüsse, Tomaten,	Peanuts, tomatoes,
Kleine, rote Kartoffeln,	Small, red potatoes,
Schöne, saftige Schinken,	Nice and juicy hams,
Und heiße, kremige Süßkartoffeln.	And hot and creamy yams.
Mohrrüben und Beete,	Carrots and beets,
Viel pikanten Aufschnitt,	Lots of spicy meats,
Popcorn und Bohnen	Popcorn and beans,
Und 'ne Platte mit Sardinen!	And a platter of sardines!

Austern und Muscheln,	Oysters and clams,
Mit süßen und sauren Marmeladen,	With sweet and sour jams,
Und Pfirsichen und Pflaumen,	And peaches and prunes,
Und den besten Makronen nur.	And only the best macaroons.

Kräcker und Käse,	Crackers and cheese,
Pudding mit Erbsen,	Pudding with peas,
Brot…Weiß und Roggen	Breads . . . white and rye,
Mit Sahne und Kürbiskuchen.	With cream and pumpkin pie.
'ne Party! 'ne Party!	A party! A party!
Wir machen 'ne Party.	We're having a party.
Wir können essen und singen,	We can eat and sing,
Und das ist alles, was ich bring'.	And that's all I will bring.

Song to Accompany Story 8

Geschenke *(Presents)*

[Sung to the melody of a Mexican folk tune]

Oma hat heut' Geburtstag.	It's our grandma's birthday.
Wir warten schon drauf,	We really can't wait
All ihre Geschenke zu sehen.	To see all her presents.
Ich wett', sie sind toll!	I bet they are great!
Unsre Freunde und Verwandten	Our friends and our family
Kommen herein.	Are coming right in.
Nun ist es soweit.	So now it is time.
Die Bescherung kann beginnen.	Let the presents begin.
Oh, Oma, wie toll!	Oh, Grandma, that's great!
Das sieht ja fein aus.	It really looks fine.
Genau, was du wolltest:	It's just what you wanted:
Ein blaues Stachelschwein!	A blue porcupine!
Oh, Oma, wie gut!	Oh, Grandma, that's good!
Welch nettes Geschenk:	The present is nice:
Ein Standbild von dir,	A statue of you
Und das ist aus Eis.	That is made out of ice.
Nun, was ist das Geschenk hier,	Now what is this present
Das so grell aussieht?	That looks very bright?
Ein dickes Känguru, das fliegen kann –	A fat kangaroo that can fly—
Ein Drachen!	It's a kite!
Und was ist das da	And what is that one
Mit der großen, gelben Schleife?	With the big yellow bow?
Ein Schweinchen aus Plastik	A plastic toy pig
Mit 'ner Nase, die glüht.	With a nose that can glow.
Die Geschenke sind nett.	The presents are nice.
Die Geschenke sind komisch.	The presents are fun.
Der Stapel wächst weiter;	The pile is growing;
Er muss ja eine Tonne wiegen.	It must weigh a ton.
Die Geschenke sind gut.	The presents are good.
Die Geschenke sind fein.	The presents are fine.
Ein Geschenk ist manchmal	A present can be
Wie ein bisschen Sonnenschein.	Like a little sunshine.

English/German Picture Dictionary

Here are some of the people, places, and things that appear in this book.

airplanes
Flugzeuge

brown
braun

bear
Bär

cake
Kuchen

blue
blau

car
Auto

bow
Schleife

clouds
Wolken

coat
Fell

feet
Füße
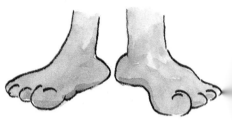

cow
Kuh

fish
Fisch

Dad
Vati

flower
Blume

door
Tür

friends
Freunde

family
Familie

frog
Frosch

garden
Garten

hat
Hut

giraffe
Giraffe

head
Kopf

Grandma
Großmutter

kitchen
Küche

hands
Hände

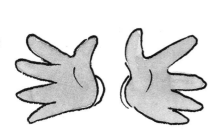

left
links

happy
glücklich

living room
Wohnzimmer

Mom
Mutti

potatoes
Kartoffeln

party
Party

presents
Geschenke

piano
Klavier

pig
Schwein

purple
lila

red
rot

pocket
Tasche

right
rechts

sad
traurig

tomatoes
Tomaten

shoes
Schuhe

toy
Spielzeug

sky
Himmel

turtle
Schildkröte

socks
Socken

world
Welt

store
Geschäft

yellow
gelb

Word List

Abenteuer
aber
alle
allermeisten
alles
als
alt
älter
am
an
Arm
auch
auf
Aufführung
aus
aussehen
Auto
Baby
bald
bei
Beinen
bekommt
besonders
besser
Besuch
Bilder
bindet
blaue
Blumen
braune
Bruder
Buch
bügelt
bürstet
dann
darüber
das
dass
dem
den
denkt
der
dich
die
doch
drei
du
eben
ein

eine
einem
einen
einkaufen
eins
Eis
entfernte
er
erinnert
es
etwas
euch
eure
Familie
fängt
Farben
fertig
fertig machen
fiel
flüstert
fragt
Frau
freue
Freunde
fröhliche
fünf
für
Garten
Gäste
Geburtstag
Geburtstags-
   party
gehen
gelben
gern
Geschäft
Geschenk
Gesicht
gibt
glücklich
große
größer
Großmutter
grünen
gut
Haare
haben
hängen
Hans

hat
hatten
Hemd
herum
Herzen
heute
hin
hinten
hinter
hoffe
holen
Hosen
Hut
ich
Idee
ihm
ihn
ihr
ihre
im
in
isst
ist
ja
Jahre
jeder
jetzt
jubeln
Kamera
Kätzchen
Katzen
kaufen
Kerzen
Kinder
klatschen
Klavier
klebt
Kleid
kleine
Knie
kommen
können
Kopf
Krawatte
Kuchen
kurze
lächelt
lachen
lange

lässt
laufen
laut
Lebens-
   geschichte
leeres
Lenkrad
letzte
lieb
liebt
Lied
lilafarbenen
links
lustig
machen
mag
malen
Maria
mich
mit
mitsingen
möchte
Morgen
Musik
Mutti
nach
nächsten
neben
nein
neue
nicht
Nikolaus
noch
nur
öffnet
orange
Orte
Parfüm
Partyhüte
passenden
Pflaster
Photo
Pinsel
Pralinen
Prinzessin
rechts
reden
reist
riecht

rosa
rote
sagen
sang
Schachtel
schauen
schenken
schenkte
schläft
schmecken
schnell
schon
Schoß
schreiben
Schuhe
schwarze
Schwester
sehen
sehr
sein
setzt
sich
sie
sieht
sind
singen
sitzen
so
sogar
sollen
Sorgen
Spaß
spielen
Spielsachen
Spielzeug
stecken
stehen
steigen
strahlen
Straße
Süßigkeiten
Tag
tanzen
Taschen
traurig
Überraschung
um
umarmt
und

unsere
unten
unter
Vati
versuchen
viel
vier
voll
von
Vorberei-
   tungen
vorne
war
was
wäscht
weil
weiß
weit
wenn
wie
wieder
will
wir
wird
Wohnzimmer
wunder-
   schönes
zählt
Zeit
zieht
Zimmer
zu
zum
zwei

Danke schön!
Ich hab' dich
   lieb.
Guten
   Morgen!
machen mit
Spaß haben
zu Hause
Alles Gute
   zum Ge-
   burtstag!